For my wonderful granddaughter,
Big Little Esty.

STERLING CHILDREN'S BOOKS
New York

An Imprint of Sterling Publishing Co., Inc.
1166 Avenue of the Americas
New York, NY 10036

STERLING CHILDREN'S BOOKS and the distinctive Sterling Children's Books logo
are registered trademarks of Sterling Publishing Co., Inc.

ISBN 978-1-4549-1906-3

Distributed in Canada by Sterling Publishing Co., Inc.
c/o Canadian Manda Group, 664 Annette Street
Toronto, Ontario, Canada M6S 2C8
Distributed in the United Kingdom by GMC Distribution Services
Castle Place, 166 High Street, Lewes, East Sussex, England BN7 1XU
Distributed in Australia by NewSouth Books, 45 Beach Street, Coogee, NSW 2034, Australia

For information about custom editions, special sales, and premium and corporate purchases,
please contact Sterling Special Sales at 800-805-5489 or specialsales@sterlingpublishing.com.

Manufactured in China

Lot #:
2   4   6   8   10   9   7   5   3   1
01/17

www.sterlingpublishing.com

Design by Heather Kelly
The artwork for this book was created using ink and watercolor

BIG
LITTLE HIPPO

BY VALERI GORBACHEV

STERLING CHILDREN'S BOOKS
New York

Little Hippo was the youngest in his family.

And very tall Giraffe, who would come to the river for a drink, was much, much bigger.

And, of course, giant Elephant was much, much, MUCH bigger.

"*Everyone* is bigger than me," grumbled Little Hippo to himself.

He was the smallest, too. His sister was bigger. His brothers were bigger. His mother was bigger. And his father was bigger.

His neighbor, big, old Crocodile,
was much bigger than Little Hippo.

"Mommy, why am I so little?" asked Little Hippo.

"Don't worry," said his mother. "You will grow up to be big just like your daddy and me."

"But I don't want to wait!" said Little Hippo. "I want to be big right *now*."

Little Hippo felt like the smallest creature in
the world as he walked between giant trees . . .

...and tall thickets of grass.

Just then Little Hippo saw a baby beetle lying
helplessly on his back.

"Poor baby! Let me help you!" said Little Hippo.

And he rolled the tiny beetle over onto his feet.

"Thank you, Big Hippo!" said the beetle's family. "You were very kind to help our baby!"

"Wow!" exclaimed Little Hippo. "They called me BIG!"
And suddenly, he *felt* very big.

"I'm big now!" cried Little Hippo,
running past giant Elephant.

"I'm big now!" cried Little
Hippo, running past tall Giraffe.

"I'm big now!" cried Little Hippo, running past big, old Crocodile.

"Mommy, I'm big now!" he cried.

And he told her all about the baby beetle he had helped.

"How wonderful!" said his mother. "You are growing up. You are *Big* Little Hippo now!"

He smiled a happy hippo smile.

His new name made him feel *just* the right size.